AGGIE AND THE CHICKEN DANCE

A Read it Again Rhyming Picture Book

EPIGRAPH: A joyful
heart is good medicine.
Proverbs 17:22
Intl. Standard Bible

SHARON L. PARKER

WESTBOW
PRESS®
A DIVISION OF THOMAS NELSON
& ZONDERVAN

DEDICATION

To my beloved Grandma Aggie...
a kindly neighbor

Hometown, Pennsylvania, that's where she was from.
Up the hill, down the hill, Aggie used to run.

She was always ready, to lend a helping hand,
To Iva, Joan, or Betty, even the plumber man.

I called her Grandma Aggie, for she was dear to me,
but some folks didn't like her. That was plain to see.
Cause Aggie had a habit of wooing silly hens,
after they had laid their eggs and roosted in their pens.
One by one, they'd listen for Aggie's special call.

Yodel-lady, Yodel-lady, Yodel-lady-oh!
Dozens came a running, through Aggie's red barn door.

Peeping, clucking, trilling chickens flew across the floor.
When Aggie started singing, they all began to prance.
Twirling, tapping, clapping, how those chickens loved to dance.

One night some sleepy farmers, heard music in the air.
"What is that noise, that chicken noise?" they clamored in despair.

Carefree, clucking chickens drove them down the hill.
Angry farmers marched right up to Aggie's red barn sill.
"What are you doing lady?" they asked in one accord.

Aggie winked, then yanked them to the party on the floor.
Once Aggie started singing, they couldn't help but prance.
Twirling, tapping clapping, how those farmers learned to dance!

When the romp was over, Aggie's tasty tarts,
called them to the kitchen. They raced with eager hearts.

After snack the farmers, with their lively hens,
danced cheek-to-cheek, back up to their cozy chicken pens.
"You'll be back tomorrow?" Aggie shouted from the door.
They did not hear, but every night the hens were back for more.

AFTERWORD

The character Aggie is based on a childhood neighbor who stood in as the author's grandmother as her mother battled cancer. "I want to honor Grandma Aggie, whose humility, nurture, and zest for life made a difference in mine." Aggie and the Chicken Dance is a zany celebration of life in a world that children sometimes find all too serious.

ABOUT THE AUTHOR

Aggie and the Chicken Dance is Sharon L. Parker's first Read it Again Rhyming Picture Book. She began writing seriously while still in college. Her hobbies include reading, singing and traveling to visit her children and grandchildren. The author believes that rhythmic storytelling is fun, adding joy to children's lives and making the pleasure of reading even more accessible.

ENDNOTES...STAY TUNED FOR MORE

FARMER – a farmer must work hard and long hours in order to produce crops and take care of livestock. There is little time for fun. Most farmers have helpers to get the work done.

CHICKENS – Chickens are domestic birds called poultry. They have small wings and heavy bodies making it hard for them to fly long distances. Domestic chickens live on farms and provide eggs for family members. Female chickens are called hens. Male chickens are called roosters. Sometimes their feathers are used for decorative purposes.

EGGS – Hens lay over 200 eggs a year, but usually slow down their laying when the weather is cold. Eggs come in many colors besides white. Some are brown, green, and blue. Fertilized eggs will grow into baby chickens. Unfertilized eggs will not.

GARDENS – Gardens are important on a farm. Vegetables used for cooking and herbs used for seasoning are grown in gardens. There are also flower gardens on farms, making them more beautiful. Sweet-smelling, colorful flowers help bees make honey.

FILL IN THE BLANKS...

A_ _ie

_ gg

C_ ick_ _

G _ _ den

A RIDDLE...

Q. Why did the egg laugh her head off?

A. Because she was eggs-terical!

KNOCK-KNOCK JOKE...

Knock-knock!

Who's there?

Hatch!

Hatch-who?

Bless you!

COLOR THE EGGS.

Can you turn them into a flower?

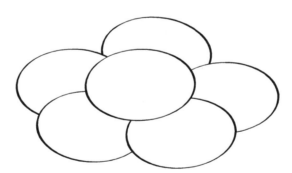

CPSIA information can be obtained
at www.ICGtesting.com
Printed in the USA
BVHW021927280719
554530BV00019B/1566/P